THE GENIE

INSATIABLE

F. SIMMONS

THE GENIE: INSATIABLE

Self-Published

Audiobook narrated by: Luna Yves

1st edition 2025

ISBN 978-1-7636313-0-4

Cover design: F Simmons

Preface

Seeker, seeker, by candle fire,

Three wishes granted, thy heart's desire,

Yet heed my words, for a wish may deceive,

Not every wish, is what it seems...

Insatiable. A life teetering on the precipice of existence, an energy too extraordinary to contain, for life is but a fleeting moment, too brief and precious to live according to someone else's design.

In a way, this brief introduction may serve as a gateway to your vulnerable heart, opening the portal to your highest potential, awakening your hidden, dormant desires, and bringing them to life in this thing we call third dimensional reality. To dream as though you are living, and to live as though you are dreaming, for the greatest manifester is the genie, and that genie resides within you...

This short tale takes place somewhere within the timeline of the third novel of the Sex God series.

Question: *What would you risk, and how deep would you surrender, to seize all that you have ever desired?*

I would like to thank Susana, Luna, Salma, Farida, Raneem, Haider, and especially Legna for accompanying me on this journey.

CHAPTER 1: TRUST

Many moons ago…

In a yet to be discovered unknown world, where the emerald, green canopies tower and toucans call in the morning skies, there lived an interestingly quirky, yet charmingly strong-willed young woman named Iara. She was unlike anyone the tribe had ever seen, having flowing, olive green hair that shimmered like the leaves above, and her skin glowed copper and brown, the same as the earth beneath her. Her brown eyes sparkled with a fierce spirit.

From a young age, Iara displayed an extraordinary talent for hunting. Amidst the dense, green jungle bed, she honed her skills, mastering the art of tracking and trapping with an agility that captivated all who bore witness. Her prowess won the admiration of her entire tribe, and even her father, the honourable chief, looked upon her with immense pride, the strength of her ancestors flowed through her.

Yet, despite her achievements, Iara carried the weight of societal expectations. At the age 31 years young, she was the eldest of her

1

sisters and yet to be married, a reality that pressed heavily upon her heart. The whispers of the tribe urged her toward marriage, a role she felt increasingly obligated to embrace. Her gaze eventually fell upon Chimba, the handsome, wealthy merchant and part-time warrior of the tribe. He seemed to possess it all; charisma, skill, rugged charm, and a future that hinted at leadership, even if he was not the chief himself.

However, doubt clouded her heart. Iara believed she stood little chance against her cousin Yurani, a younger, more feminine woman who by all standards the tribespeople raved of her unending beauty, appeared to be more his type. The thought of competing for Chimba's affection filled her with unease, and she found herself at a crossroads, torn between the hunter she was... and the woman she was expected to become...

I n the midst of her daily activities, Iara moved slowly through the busy village centre. Laughter rang out as the air was filled with the sounds of trade and the fragrant smoke of cooking fires. The tribes folk rejoiced, for the men had returned from distant lands, bearing spoils of victory from a recent conquest. With stealth and cunning, they returned from the lands of another tribe, where the game roamed freely under the watchful eye of the gods. And lo, the hunt was fruitful, for many birds were taken by their arrows, and the jungle deer fell before their might. Thus, laden with the spoils of their transgression, they arrived bearing a feast that was rich and plentiful. Yet, an uneasy sensation swelled within Iara, a feeling that watchful eyes were upon her.

Abruptly, as if stirred by an unseen force, she turned sharply, her heart quickening. In that moment, a stranger emerged from the swarm, his presence commanding, mysterious. He bore features of a distant land, his face unlike any of her people, and she found herself wary, and yet intensely curious.

"My lady, art thou… *Ee-Ya-Ra*?" he inquired with a deep voice.

Taken aback, she regarded him with caution. Who was this man, so striking and outlandish? "I am she, and what do you seek stranger?" she replied.

"Take my hand," he called, offering his palm, inviting her in as if there were more promise.

Iara was not one to leap into the unknown without careful deliberation; she was wise and guarded, her judgment keen and unclouded. She was not naive, nor easily trusting, as was the job of the eldest sibling. As she observed the stranger before her, she remained cautious. It was as if he possessed an intimate knowledge of her, arousing both intrigue and nervousness all at the same time.

Her thoughts were caught in a frenzy. What would the townsfolk think if she accepted his hand? The gossipy nature of her people was well known, and she could already envision the wild tales that would emerge about her and this foreign figure. The very act of grasping his hand could ignite a storm of speculation, a trivial gesture that could be blown to scandalous proportions.

And yet, to refuse his offer entirely would invite a different kind of scrutiny, one that suggested a reluctance to engage. She felt the uncertainty surrounding her grow. At last, with a bewildered and confused look, she extended her hand. The stranger grasped her palm tightly, drawing her closer with a force that sent a shiver coursing through her body. In that moment, Iara stood on the edge of an adventure she had never imagined.

"Come, follow me," he urged. "I possess something of great importance!"

"Who are you, and to where do you lead me?" she queried curiously.

The stranger responded gently, with words flowing:

Down by the river, I shall show you the way,

To a glade bathed in light, where the waters cascade,

There, where the crystal currents gently glide,

And all that you seek will be yours to decide

Yet as they ventured further from the crowds, Iara felt a sense of worry blossom within. Each step away from the familiar heightened her senses. It was a curious turmoil; she sensed a hint of trust toward this stranger, yet the rational part of her heart cautioned against such foolishness. Would this path lead her to fortune, or disaster? The conflict waged within, both frightening and exciting her spirit.

As if reading her mind, the stranger halted abruptly, releasing Iara's hand from his grasp. With a swift movement, he leapt backward, spinning upon his heels, and arms outstretched, his wide smile etched upon his face.

"Why do you halt? What sorcery unfolds before me? Speak, I implore you!" Iara exclaimed with irritation.

"My lady," the stranger replied, "in this moment, I present unto you a choice. You may return to your tribe, to the familiar, to the only place you have ever known. I do not seek to hinder your path. Yet, forgive me, for your surprise awaits just beyond the horizon."

"I know you not, nor do you know me!" Iara retorted hesitantly.

"If I might hazard a guess, you are a woman of curiosity, are you not?" he continued, his gaze piercing through her guard. "The one who yearns for adventure, a break from the mundane. After all, you are an adept huntress, moving among the males of your kin. Surely your spirit cannot rest without uncovering the unknown, the elusive catch that lies in wait!"

"I do enjoy a surprise or two," she conceded, though a sense of duty tugged at her heart. "Yet I have errands to attend. My family shall soon seek me, and I must gut the fish and prepare the evening meal."

"Indeed, those qualities you possess are truly endearing, reflecting the essence of your character," the stranger remarked. "Iara, I shall not detain you for long. I assure you, it will be but a brief moment, after which you may return to your family, your spirit uplifted by the precious gift I wish to bestow upon you."

"I… I cannot, but I thank you regardless," Iara cautiously replied, her curiosity making it hard to find the right words.

"As you desire, Iara," he responded with a warm smile, "I trust the remainder of your day will be filled with happiness.. and light."

With that, Iara turned and began her walk home. However, as she progressed, she felt compelled to look back, her heart still doubtful. The stranger's figure receded into the distance, his presence diminishing like a fading memory. Had she made the right decision?

With each step, her hesitation grew heavier. As she cast another glance over her shoulder, she spotted him in the distance, faintly gathering his belongings. Her heart quickened. What gift might lie hidden within the promise he proposed?

"Wait!" Iara yelled loudly, breaking the silence.

She began to jog toward him, as if pulled by a magnetic force. "Come on, make haste!" he amusingly urged. Iara chased after him as he smiled, his pace brisk as he was walking away.

The river finally came into view, its shiny surface glistening under the jungle sun.

"Well, stranger," Iara said, her breath coming in quick bursts, "now that we are here, spill it. Tell me, what you have brought me here for?"

"Iara," he replied, "do you believe in fate?"

She regarded him with a puzzled expression. "I do, and?"

"Do you believe in the possibility of… a miracle?" he asked, his eyes sparkling with intensity.

Iara let out a raucous laughter. "Ye," Iara replied, "but what of it? Miracles are as rare as the explosion of a distant star!"

The stranger continued without a misstep. "Do you believe, that if one desires something so fervently, harnessing the right energy, loyalty, commitment and prayer, that they shall ultimately attain their desires?"

"Well," Iara responding thoughtfully, "eventually, they will be closer to it than if they had done nothing at all!"

"Lo! Herein lies my purpose," he declared boldly. "I have come to grant thy wishes, though not simply with the snap of my fingers. I seek to disrupt your daily habits, and to infuse your quiet, ordinary life with a hint of excitement! If only for a fleeting moment."

"Wait, what do you speak of?" Iara inquired curiously. "What is your name, stranger?"

"I am Uriel, from the distant land of Ur. Yet tonight, I have come to render my service unto thee! I am your genie, oh Iara, at your command, here to fulfill all that you wish... and all that you desire."

"Is this, some kind of game?" Iara replied with deep scepticism. "Let me understand this clearly: a strange man emerges from the depths of nowhere, knows my name, my preferences, knows things about me that no stranger should, and yet I am to place my trust in thee?"

"Does it not seem to be the very essence of a genie, destined by the stars themselves?" Uriel countered without hesitation. "You are not naive, Iara," he continued, acknowledging her nature. "It has served you well thus far. Very well, indeed. I have chosen you to be the beneficiary of my gifts. Thus! Request me three wishes, and three wishes I shall grant!"

"And what, pray tell, is the catch?" Iara replied, crossing her arms and a playful grin widening upon her lips. "Everything comes at a price. State thy purpose!"

Uriel began gently, taking a deep breath, before sharing, "In these lands, I find but a brief moment to rest before I continue my journey. Yet let it be known that in every village, and in every town I visit, where I engage with the people, even the simplest suggestion can light the way for those who are lost. Each act of kindness serves as a drop of hope in life's vast ocean, and the smallest gesture can produce the greatest ripple. You, Iara, possess the power to create such ripples. So, when you wonder why, know that it is in my nature: your success and your joy shall bring my own, and that is the payment that I seek."

Iara gazed at the stranger in cryptic fashion, pondering the mystery he presented.

"However, Oh Iara, I must warn thee," Uriel uttered:

Call to me, and I shall heed,

Your every want, your every need,

Your heart's truest wish, I shall grant,

Anything you desire, just take my hand,

Yet there is only one, a wish forbidden,

Not every wish can be fulfilled and written

She turned her gaze to Uriel, a little confused. "What do you mean, one wish is forbidden?" she asked curiously, her eyes searching for the answer.

Uriel chuckled softly. He stepped closer, the air around him shifting. "You are granted the power to summon me for absolutely any request in this known universe, but one wish, Oh Iara, can never be yours to command!"

The words seemed to stand on the tip of his tongue, something hidden beneath layers of mystery. She anxiously took a step forward, her fingers twitching, struggling to grasp the truth that he so carefully held beyond her reach.

"And what is it, Uriel? What is this *'thing'* thou art withholding from me?" Iara nervously asked.

Uriel's laughter spilled from his lips. "You shall know, in time, sweet Iara," he spoke. "But I cannot speak of it, for it is not a matter of words. It is a feeling, a knowing that will awaken within you when the moment comes. You will know… when you know."

Iara's heart fluttered. She could not grasp the meaning of his words, yet his cryptic reply left her open to more.

"Patience, Iara," he muttered. "Your heart shall know, and when it does, surely, you shall understand."

Uriel continued gently, "I shall not delay you any longer; you are free to forge your own path. However, if you find yourself drawn to what I offer, I invite you to return here at eleven minutes past the eleventh hour, when the night is at its zenith, and all the villagers have settled into their slumber. Bring with you a lit candle, your open heart, and the wish you long to manifest upon your lips. I will be here every night, waiting patiently until you are armed with your wish in mind. Until then, oh Iara."

Iara stood there, her mind swirling with confusion. Just then, Uriel began to remove his shirt, leaving her uncertain about where to direct her gaze. Struggling with modesty, yet curious, she could not help but take in the sight of his bare torso, defined, and glistening in the sunlight.

"Do you see something you like?" Uriel teased playfully.

Without hesitation, he leaped into the cool waters of the river, sending ripples across the surface, and lightly splashing Iara with the mist. Iara felt a flush rise to her cheeks, caught flustered and embarrassed. As she turned to make her way back to the village, her heart raced with a momentous decision ahead of her. Would she return to meet him, that stranger in the woods, or choose the comfort of her familiar life?

Later that night, Iara found herself lost in thought, grappling with the absurdity of her dilemma. Why would she place her trust in a stranger like Uriel, who claimed to be a genie? Yet the pull of curiosity was too strong to resist, and the fear of missing out loomed large. What if he truly possessed the power he spoke of?

If it was all a lie, at least it was something out of the ordinary. Thus, Iara committed to return, though doubt continued to tear at her with relentless force. She wrapped her hunters blade with care, tucking it against her hip beneath her skirt, ensuring it was well concealed in case danger lurked in the shadows, and naturally, a stranger was not to be trusted. Armed with a candle that Uriel advised her to bring, she made her way back to the river, the meeting place Uriel had promised for the dead of night, when all stood still.

As Iara approached the designated meeting spot, a cold shiver caused the hairs on the back of her neck to stand on end. She began to question her sanity. Was it reckless to venture into the dark of night alone, drawn by the promise of a stranger she had met the very same day? Had she truly lost her mind? Bold and strong-willed, she usually embraced challenges with courage, yet this felt alarmingly out of character. Still, the burning curiosity propelled her onward.

Soon, she glimpsed Uriel's shadow, faint against the moonless sky. He knelt on the ground, his form embodying a peaceful meditation.

"Iara, you have arrived right on time," Uriel said, a smile warming his features.

"I… I have," she stammered, momentarily taken aback by his calm energy.

He gestured for her to come forward, then carefully took the lit candle she carried and placed it between them, its flame illuminating their faces.

"Now, Iara, you come with an open heart and the words of your first wish upon your lips?"

"Of course," she replied firmly. "There is no other reason for me to be here."

"Then, may I ask you to share with me what lies within?" he urged gently.

"Well, Uriel," she began, her voice barely a whisper, swallowed by the clicking of cicadas in the jungle landscape. "The truth is, I already possess many skills that bring me contentment in this life. I aid the village in foraging and building our huts, carrying forth the knowledge and wisdom passed down by the elders. I can craft weapons and create art that reflects our culture. We are simple people, not longing for the riches that grand civilisations may offer. Yet, what I truly yearn for… is to embrace the essence of femininity within me, and the deep longing for love."

Uriel, out of nowhere, let out a deep, thunderous boom:

Speak your command, and I shall fuel your fire,

I will give you whatever you want, whatever you desire,

In spirit, I shape, in flesh, it shall be,

For reality shall bend to your will and your plea

The candle extinguished abruptly, as though his words had caused the very air to change.

"So, Uriel, let it be this…"

Oh Uriel, hear my plea, I wish… to be with Chimba!

"That he shall regard me more favourably than any woman he has ever laid eyes upon, that he may choose me, and I may find love, finally."

Uriel's expression shifted in seriousness, his eyes narrowing. "Oh, Iara, are you certain? I must express that wishing for a certain '*kind*' of person, with particular charming qualities, could bring a favourable result. Yet to wish for a '*specific*' individual is a dangerous path, for it encroaches upon that persons free will. Are you absolutely sure?"

"Uriel!" she challenged, "are you certain you possess the power to deliver? Or are you merely finding an excuse? Are you a deceiving charlatan of a genie, perchance?"

"Never, not in a million moons!" he replied unwaveringly. "I am here to fulfill your bidding; your every wish is my command. Anything you desire, simply command me, and I shall oblige."

"But before I grant this wish," he added, "I must inquire further about this man. The more I know, the stronger the fulfillment of your wish may be. May I?"

"What would you like to know?" Iara nervously replied.

"Tell me more about this man," Uriel urged. "What makes him so special?"

Iara paused, gathering her thoughts. "Well, there are many things. I have known him since childhood, and I cherish the memories of our days as children. Yet as we grew older, we drifted apart, only ever exchanging nods in passing. He married young, and he is loyal, oh so handsome, charming, and intelligent, he possesses it all. To be honest, perhaps I relish the hunt, because it grants me a chance to be near him. Though we hardly ever share the same hunting party, I hope that one day, no other women will be present, and I may steal a moment alone with him. But alas, I have had no fortune thus far. He probably would not fancy me anyway; I am much too rugged."

"Is this man, by chance, still bound by marriage?" Uriel inquired, a note of judgement in his tone. "Is that not a trivial matter?"

"I would not say so," Iara replied firmly. "His previous wife cannot bear him any children, and thus he seeks a companion worthy to bear him offspring."

"Tell me," Uriel pressed sincerely, "why must you have him? What is it that you cannot achieve alone, right now?"

Iara hesitated, her thoughts swirling. "Oh Uriel, my duties reign heavily upon me. Perhaps it is my nature, and I grow anxious in his presence. My heart shudders, yet I am not skilled in the art of sensuality. I am too practical... or maybe I have simply become that way."

"I will ask you one last time," Uriel insisted. "Are you certain this shall be your wish?"

"More than anything," Iara confessed with increasing determination.

"Then, thy wish is my command. Come, kneel before me."

Iara knelt opposite Uriel. "Light the candle once more," he instructed. She obeyed, the slithering flame casting a warm glow around them.

"Now, before we proceed, Iara," Uriel said softly, "I ask of you one thing. The truth is, that what you communicate may not hold the utmost importance. What truly matters… is that which lies within your heart, what you feel deep within, and what dwells in your subconscious. For this to manifest, I demand you to trust me utterly, absolutely. I am here to serve you."

"Before I bestow my trust upon you," Iara replied, her eyebrow raised, "what is the catch? What is it that you desire from me? Why not the other tribes folk?"

Uriel's expression grew serious. "My time is limited. I am but a vessel, unable to grant wishes to every single soul. Yet you, dear Iara, were called to me. Something beyond this realm directed me to you, and I only accept the path in which I am needed. If you did not require my aid, I would not stand before you, would I not?"

Iara gazed intently into Uriel's eyes, searching for even a modicum of suspicion. Yet, he appeared as clear as day; she witnessed a man who was entirely convinced of his own words.

"For whatever reason, Uriel, I trust you with all my heart," she firmly declared.

Uriel took a deep breath, inhaling the air around him, and slowly exhaling, "Oh Iara, your wish is my command."

Your trust in me makes this manifestation stronger,

Thy wish be granted, your wish to conquer,

Spoken forth your desire, it shall be yours,

Once received, you shall yearn for more...

"Now, look deeply into my eyes!" Uriel commanded, in a bellowing voice.

As Iara fixed her eyes upon him, she beheld a sight unlike any she had encountered. It was as if she were peering into the very depths of a bottomless abyss, a speeding cosmos of mysteries. The intensity of his stare drew her in, a magnetic pull leaving her breathless.

In that moment, the world around her began to blur, her sight dizzying and fading into oblivion. All at once, her world went dark...

THE GENIE: INSATIABLE

CHAPTER 2: VULNERABILITY

I ara, feeling dazed, stirred from her slumber, roused by the clamorous sounds echoing outside her humble dwelling. For reasons unknown, she found herself unusually tired, having slept late into the morning, a rarity for one so accustomed to the early light of day. Though fatigue overwhelmed her entire body, everything else appeared as it should, the world outside carrying on just like any other day.

Determined to revitalise her spirit, she approached the basin of cool water, preparing to splash her face, as was her daily ritual. Yet, as she peered into the surface, an unexpected sight greeted her. The reflection that stared back seemed subtly altered, a hint of something extraordinary shimmering in her appearance. Her skin radiated with an ethereal glow, a quality she could not quite discern but felt deeply within her.

After adorning herself with her usual attire, the weight of her hunter's knife resting upon her thigh and her bow and arrows secured at her side, she ventured into the heart of the village. However, a peculiar sensation washed over her as she navigated through the crowd of people. Many eyes were upon her, and she did not seem to know why.

A rush of shyness overtook Iara, and she attempted to dismiss the feeling, pressing onward toward the jungle where the hunting party awaited. As was tradition, they divided into smaller groups, each prepared for the day's pursuit. The hunting parties were soon being assigned, and Chimba, the esteemed leader of the warriors, stepped forward with a commanding presence. Iara felt her breath hitch in her throat once more; for so long, he was the man of her dreams, a figure of everything.

Chimba was a man larger than most in his tribe, yet surprisingly agile. His strong, dense frame built from years of hunting in the jungle. His long, thick braided hair wrapped tightly, and his face bore a flat nose, reshaped from many battles.

"Listen well, my friends," Chimba declared with authority. "We shall embark on a fruitful hunt this morning. All are to venture westward, toward the mountain ridge, for I have heard whispers of a bountiful gathering of Chacoan peccaries!"

As the warriors broke into their usual groups, Iara felt a stir of excitement within. The hunting party needed a bountiful catch for the evening feast and the remainder of the week, but to her astonishment, Chimba's eyes fell upon her. "This time, Iara shall accompany me," he announced. "I wish to determine if her skills are as worthy as others have claimed!"

Shock coursed through Iara; never had she ventured into the wild with Chimba, especially not in such an intimate setting.

As they traversed the dense jungle, with the sounds of chirping birds and rustling leaves, an unusual quiet engulfed the space between them. The loudness of the jungle seemed to fade into the distance, leaving only the soft crunch of foliage beneath their feet. It felt as though an eternity passed in silence until Chimba the warrior, finally turned to her.

"Iarita," he said, invoking her childhood name, an endearing title that brought forth a rush of memories. "Oh, how good it is to finally speak with you once more!"

Iara blinked, momentarily taken aback. "Huh? What is it, Chimba?"

"I apologise for the time that has slipped by without our words shared," he continued, his tone growing sombre. "You know... I had found my wife, and that was partly the reason for my silence."

"Yes, of course," Iara replied, trying to mask her disappointment. "I am sure it was; you did not wish to stray from her. I completely understand."

Chimba's expression turned sincere, his eyes gathering in intensity. "But, in all honesty, Iara, you have occupied my thoughts for the last decade. You have lingered upon my mind."

Iara's heart raced, surprise, and confusion washing over her. "Huh? This is news to me. What do you mean? Not once have you looked my way all these years!"

"I have told you before, I had a wife," he replied over.

"Yet I have seen you converse easily with other women," she countered in raised suspicion. "You seemed untroubled by it." The tension hung between them, a moment of unspoken feelings.

"Iarita," Chimba began, "the honest truth, is that I could not speak to you, for in reality, I hold you in higher regard than all others. Truth be told, even during the time with my wife, the thought of conversing with you filled me with guilt. Because my mind should have been focused solely on her.. and yet, it was not. Iarita, I wish to ask for your forgiveness."

Iara's heart pounded, shock flooding her body. This was the moment she had longed for, the culmination of dreams that now laid before her. Yet, it felt surreal, almost too immediate.

As though all the years of lost time between them had vanished from her mind, without hesitation, she replied, "Of course, Chimba. I understand… everything; I forgave you many years ago."

Then, in the thick of lush jungle, surrounded by a noisy raucous, they moved closer and exchanged a kiss, a connection physical that conveyed years of missed opportunities, forgiveness, and the possibilities that lay ahead.

The following night, whilst the moon brightly guided the jungles path, Iara returned to the same riverbank where she had been charmed the night before. This time, a new light had entered her step, as though the very air she breathed, was imbued with an invisible force that carried her forward. Her eyes, brighter than ever before, sought the familiar figure that she felt she had known for a lifetime.

There he was, as though conjured by her very will, summoned as if by sheer magic. Uriel, still in the same place, kneeling in his calm meditation. His presence was peaceful, yet something in the air trembled, and she could not place a finger on it.

Iara's mind was in absolute fantasy. The man of her dreams, her soul's most secret desire, had finally taken notice of her. Even the radiant Yurani, who seemed to embody youthful, timeless beauty, could not claim his attention as she just had. It was as if fate had guided him to her, and she, in her heart, could not fathom how, nor why it had come to pass. But so it happened, the one whose voice she had longed to hear, who had haunted her thoughts, now within her grasp.

Uriel's voice drifted toward her. "Oh, Iara," he said, his gaze lifting from the river's edge to meet hers. "There is something… different within you this eve. Your every step, your glowing appearance, there is a new light upon you. What news do you have for me? Tell me, sweet one, what has come to pass?"

Iara, for a moment, hesitated. There were many thoughts rushing through her mind, but the most pressing was a release of the judgment she had held.

With a shy, trembling breath, she spoke "I… I must apologise, Uriel," she said, her eyes dropping for a moment. "For the thoughts I held before. You asked me once if I believed in miracles… And now, I see. Yes, I do, with certainty. Yesterday afternoon, a miracle came to pass, a truth made flesh in this very world. And let me tell thee, oh magic boy, you are all that you claim to be!'

A subtle grin, bright and mischievous, spread across Uriel's lips. Moonlight shone in his eyes, and he rose slowly, fluidly. "A miracle, you say?" he replied. "Then it seems I am yet a part of your fate, though I know not whether I am the cause, or the consequence. But I am glad to know that you have seen what I knew to be true. The magic, it lives within you also, Iara."

A strange warmth washed over her, a tremor of anticipation. Uriel softly smiled. "I am glad you have attained that which you sought. But tell me, what brings you to me this night? Do you have your second wish ready upon your lips?"

Iara's eyes burned with intention. "Indeed, Uriel, I have come for more!"

Uriel's smile deepened, and with a playful bow of his head, "Then, as your humble servant of desires, speak your command, O Iara... and yet, once more, I must caution thee," Uriel declared calmly,

Call to me, and I shall heed,

Your every want, your every need,

Your heart's truest wish, I shall grant,

Anything you desire, just take my hand,

Yet there is only one, a wish forbidden,

Not every wish can be fulfilled and written

Iara's eyebrow raised, a frustration beginning to settle within her. She had come to trust Uriel's wisdom, but his cryptic speech vexed her spirit. She had listened too long to his riddles, and now her patience wore thin.

"Speak plainly, Uriel," she said impatiently. "I am weary of your games. Tell me, what is this forbidden wish?"

"As I have said it before," Uriel uttered, "you shall know when the time comes, for the knowledge of it is not understood in words, but in the knowing of the heart. It is not utterance that shall reveal it, but the *'feeling'* of it, when the moment is near. When you are meant to understand, your heart will guide you."

A chill crept upon her, and a sense of confusion settled deep within her breast. What was it he had meant? And with that, Uriel's voice thundered once more, a deep and commanding tone, echoing through the night:

Speak your command, and I shall fuel your fire,

I will give you whatever you want, whatever you desire.

In spirit, I shape, in flesh, it shall be,

For reality shall bend to your will and your plea.

Iara stood before Uriel, her eyes clouded with uncertainty, "Truth be told, Uriel," she began, "I have long desired to be a mother, yet I know not if it is within my reach. My years have passed, and though once I lay with another man many years ago, the fruit of my womb did not take root. I do not know why I voice this now, but hear me, O Uriel! Let it be as I wish. Let it be this…" Her voice quivered as she spoke the words that had long remained hidden.

"Oh Uriel, hear my plea, I wish… I wish to be a mother."

Her heartbeat wildly as her command echoed into the night. Uriel's stare was piercingly mysterious. He inhaled deeply, as if drawing in the very energy of the river surrounding them, and exhaling slowly, his chest rising… and falling. As he began to speak, his voice rumbled through the silence.

"Oh Iara," he said, "thy wish is mine to grant."

Your trust in me makes this manifestation stronger,

Thy wish be granted, your wish to conquer,

Spoken forth your desire, it shall be yours,

Once received, you shall yearn for more…

As his words settled into the night, the earth beneath them seemed to shudder, as though the world itself were bending to his command. A great tremor filled the air, and once more, Iara's vision darkened… her world, as had happened before, fading to black.

The Genie: Insatiable

CHAPTER 3: ALL OR NOTHING

One wish is forbidden, a perilous game,
Speak not its name, lest you kindle its flame

L o, as the weeks passed, the morning came upon Iara like a storm of sickness. She lay in her bed, reluctant to leave its comfort for several days, for she knew not the cause of her suffering. Yet even as her body trembled with unease, her heart burned with a yearning she could not contain.

The night had been meant to be magical, but instead, she found herself making a decision she could not understand, a choice she now regretted. For years, Iara had been consumed by a love for a man who haunted her thoughts, his presence intoxicating. But once she finally had him, it felt as though everything she had imagined... had crumbled into something so hollow. It was as if her mind had deceived her, and the man she had fantasised within her thoughts... was nowhere to be seen in the man she had spent the night with countless nights ago.

She could not wait till nightfall to seek Uriel once more. There were questions racing in her mind, and her soul could not rest until they were all but answered. She had to know. She had to understand what had transpired between them, what forces had stirred within her, what magic had touched her life.

As she approached the river's edge, her eyes swept across the water… and there he was, Uriel, gathering his belongings. His silhouette was surrounded by the soft light of the morning, moving slow and meticulous, as though he were preparing to depart from this place that had become their meeting ground. There beside him was a companion she had not seen before, a chestnut horse with a sleek coat, quietly grazing along the river's edge.

"Uriel, where are you going?" She called out. "I beg your forgiveness for my absence, for I have been unwell these past few weeks," she said with regret. "Do we not yet have one final wish left, a promise unfulfilled?"

Uriel turned toward her, his expression calm, yet there was a glint of mischief in his eyes. "Oh, Iara, I am not but some spirit who lingers by the waters, waiting on your every whim. A man of flesh and blood must seek sustenance, as you know, and now and again, entertain his impulses," he responded, winking in a playful manner. "Now tell me, what have you to say that could not wait until tonight?"

Iara stood there for a moment. She opened her mouth, but the words caught in her throat. How could she explain it? How could she speak the truth that had blossomed so unexpectedly within her?

"Uriel..." Her voice faltered, but she pressed on, for there was no turning back now. "I... I am with child."

Her words stood still, as she searched his face, desperate for some sign of what he would say, of how he would respond.

Uriel's expression, however, did not change. His eyes narrowed for a brief moment, and then, with certainty, he spoke. "As you have desired, thus, your wish has been made manifest. Was it not your desire to become a mother? Was it not your wish that called forth this creation?"

Iara's pulse quickened, and a knot twisted in her stomach. She took a step forward, her voice barely a whisper, trembling. "But Uriel, did you... did you, by any chance, impregnate me?"

Her words had caught him off guard, and Uriel's eyes widened in astonishment. The question struck him like a bolt of lightning, a jolt of pure, unspoken confusion. He recoiled slightly, baffled at her response.

Uriel looked on in disbelief as he stared at Iara confused. "What? Had I fathered your child, you would have known it, would you not? Did you not spend time with Chimba?"

Iara's chest pounded, her eyes searching his, yet she kept steady, despite the turmoil within. "Yes, I spent time with him," she confessed, her gaze lowering for a moment. "But what you did not know, Uriel, is that Chimba may be impotent. He was once married, and his wife bore him no children. Perhaps... perhaps it is he who is not capable."

A moment of silence passed, before Uriel eventually responded. "It is not my place to indulge in such idle gossip, Iara, but perhaps it was not him, but his wife who could not bear children." Uriel's eyes began to lighten. "But fear not, Iara, for I am certain you will make a wonderful mother. You have the heart for it, even more so than you do as a sister, and as a hunter. You were destined for such a supreme role."

Iara's heart laid bare at his words, yet a darker question remained within, one she could not fully suppress. "How? How could this have happened? You said you could not make me pregnant, did you not?"

Uriel let out a gentle laugh, as though the matter were of little consequence. "Ah, Iara, thou art right," he said. "And know this, I cannot fulfill that wish myself, for to do so would be to grant you... two wishes in a single stroke!" he added playfully, winking in his mischief.

Iara's eyes flashed in frustration. She was not in the mood for jest, not now. There were too many emotions swirling within her, a storm she could not calm. "Oh, Uriel!" she snapped sharply. "You are not a genie, are you?"

Uriel paused in contemplation, his fingers mindlessly fidgeting with the objects he had gathered, "Indeed, you are right," he admitted. "I have been… exposed, I suppose. You have uncovered my true nature."

A shadow passed over Iara's face, and her voice grew colder, more uncertain. "Then tell me, Uriel, who are you? What are you? If not a deceiver, a manipulator, then what is it that you seek to gain from me?"

Uriel locked eyes with Iara's, and for the first time, there was a sense of something more genuine in his stare. An honesty, perhaps, or the raw truth of his own complexity. He took a deep breath, his hands relaxing as he spoke. "Now, now, Iara," he said calmly. "A manipulator seeks to control, to twist the heart, to use another for their own gain. But I… I gave thee the very wish you did request. Did I not?"

Iara's mind raced as she considered his words. The questions she had asked, the wishes she had made, had all been granted, without conditions. At least, not yet. Still, she could not rid herself of the doubt within.

"Yes," she replied quietly, still uncertain, "you have."

Uriel's eyes darkened. "So then, Iara, what deception have I played upon you?" His stare penetrated hers, as if seeking to snatch the very depths of her soul.

Iara felt the walls she had so carefully constructed around her heart began to crumble. She knew she could not hide the truth forever, though a part of her longed to do so.

"Oh Uriel, I say unto you, you have indeed granted me all that I desired, or so it seemed. Yet, though I have received much, even with Chimba, my soul finds no peace, and I find that what I truly seek... what I truly need...is not with him" Iara confessed.

"If anything, Uriel," she regrettably began, "you have come only to leave another broken heart in your wake." Uriel was taken aback by Iaras sudden confessions, uncertain how to react.

"Oh Uriel, what are you? I need to know," she whispered. "Are you a spirit? A man? A genie, a devil perhaps?"

He stepped a little closer, his voice undeniably potent. "I am neither man nor beast," he spoke, "neither good nor evil." He paused before continuing, his voice deepening;

I am your truest mirror, your deepest reflection,

All that you desire to manifest, your soul's truest connection,

Your grandest dreams and your darkest fears,

I serve as your guide, beyond all frontiers.

A shiver ran down Iara's spine, and for a moment, she was silent, trying to comprehend the enormity of it all. "But what does that mean, Uriel?" she asked, her voice trembling. "Pray, tell me. It is the least you can do."

Uriel's behaviour relaxed more so, and without another word, he took her hands gently into his.

"Iara," he began, "there is much to explain, and so little time to do so. But hear me now, for the truth is both simpler... and more complicated than you may think."

He inhaled another slow, deliberate breath, before continuing, "I am no genie, nor am I spirit," Uriel declared, staring intently. "Yet, none of what I have spoken has been false. I made a vow, Iara, to serve you, as your guide, to grant that which your heart so desires, but only if you place your trust in me, in totality, bare your naked soul, and expose your every vulnerability." His words were delicate, unmistakable, drawing her in closer, pulling her in. "And you, dear one, have done so. So now, I will share with you... my truth."

Iara tilted her head in curiosity. "How did you come so far?" she asked.

"I am Uriel!" he bellowed, "Hailing from the grand metropolis of Ur! The epicentre of the world! I was soon bound as a slave in the temple of the mighty goddess Ishtaar! In a place far, far from here. I have escaped, and I have fled, and in doing so, I have earned the wrath of all the gods... and the hatred of kingdoms both great and small!" His confession came like wildfire.

Iara's heart fluttered, her mind racing to understand. To grasp the full meaning of his presence here, in this moment. "So," Iara asking out of curiosity, "you were gifted the powers to grant wishes by the temple of Ishtaar?"

Uriel gently smiled, yet there was something in else his eyes, something haunting, that made her question whether he was truly free of the chains that bound him. "Not exactly so," he replied. "Within her temple, I learned the tantalising ways of sensuality, the mysteries of the flesh and soul, of pleasure and pain, of the forces that bind us all together. Yet, what we do here, what you and I have shared. Magic as you call it, is not of Ishtaar's doing. I am well-travelled, and in my journeys, I became a student of Hypnos, the god of slumber. Through his teachings, I learned the art of hypnosis, the power to bend minds and desires to the will."

She gasped, her breath halting as his words reached her ears, her body tingling with the heat of presence. His words rolled off the tongue ever so smoothly, and yet, there was something deeper, something darker in them, a warning maybe.

Uriel's eyes darkened, and he stepped even closer, until the space between them all but vanished. "Every wish you make, Iara, is a door opened, and a path closed. To gain everything, you must first be willing to let it all slip away." With Uriel, there was no easy way forward, no simple answer. To claim her desires, she would have to surrender much, perhaps everything.

Her heart pounded fiercely, caught between the pull of Uriel's promise, and the fear of what it might cost. She stood before him, her soul naked.

"My dearest Iara," he continued, "by now, if you do not believe in the hand of fate, then ponder the miracle that does allow two souls to find each other amid such chaos. In this endless universe, where stars shimmer and galaxies spin, the odds of two, lonely hearts converging are as rare as spotting a shooting star in the middle of a bright morning."

"Pray tell, how many galaxies do you suppose there be?" Uriel asked.

"I know not, perchance millions!" Iara mused, her eyes drifting into the cosmos.

"And within these myriad galaxies, and the countless stars that shine with brilliance, within them, how many do you reckon, sweet Iara?"

"Indeed, so many that our minds cannot grasp their numbers, not until the very end of infinity!" she replied in wonder.

"And lo, out of all these radiant stars," Uriel continued passionately, "how many planets do you think do perfectly circle their suns? How many are placed just so, with atmospheres so pure that life may flourish?"

"Only this planet that we know of, oh Uriel, and perhaps also, the realms of the gods, the heavens," she whispered softly.

"Exactly so," he affirmed. "And upon this mortal earth, the cradle of humanity, how many souls do you think have walked these earthen grounds, and how many more shall tread its path in years yet to come?"

"I come from a humble tribe, and my journeys have been few," Iara replied. "But I would guess many, indeed."

"Billions! I dare say," Uriel responded, intensity growing with each word. "And in the never-ending span of time and existence, through the endless years and months, the passing weeks, the precious days, and the coming hours, do you not see how sacred these moments are? To have shared these very brief, fleeting moments with you on this earth, is a treasure beyond compare!"

His stare bore into her soul. "Consider the impossible improbability of our meeting! To meet you, against all odds, feels like the most wondrous adventure of them all! We are not even a speck of dust in the atmosphere, not even a drop in the ocean. Is it not evident that our union is ordained? A divine miracle, indeed."

"In this moment, you and I, I and you, are but an extraordinary union within the endless cycle of existence," he continued, his eyes gleaming. "Do you not feel the divinity of this hour, Iara?"

"Uriel," she commenced, yet she faltered, uncertain. The words trembled upon her lips, but she kept them sealed. How could she ask such a thing? And yet… there was part of her that longed to.

Uriel leaned closer, his breath mingling with hers, the warmth of his presence upon her. "Now, most beautiful Iara," he whispered, "what is thy last wish?"

A tear escaped her eye, struggling to roll down her cheek. Without thought, Iara's palm came up, striking sharply across Uriel's face. But even as the sting of her slap marked his skin, the floodgates of her tears poured forth.

Uriel, unflinching, looked into her eyes, his expression calm. "Such is the law of polarity," he said. "To possess is to lack, and to desire is to be emptied, once that desire is fulfilled."

He paused, then continued, "Remember, your final wish shall be granted by the candle fire. However, Oh Iara, I must warn thee for the very last time," Uriel muttered:

Call to me, and I shall heed,

Your every want, your every need,

Your heart's truest wish, I shall grant,

Anything you desire, just take my hand,

Yet there is only one, a wish forbidden,

Not every wish can be fulfilled and written

"Yea, yea, the forbidden wish you speak of in riddles yet cannot thou clarify! I know, I know! I shall not utter its words, though I know not what they are, verily!" she spoke in frustration.

"Yet lo! I have a sneaking suspicion that you do know, Iara," Uriel replied with keen discernment. "For if you were to speak this forbidden wish aloud, then perhaps your coming here would be in vain. But if you still wish to make your third wish, return to me tomorrow tonight, and I will be waiting at the peak of the full moon."

Iara's eyes locked with his in silence, caught between the realms of the seen, and the unseen.

Uriel nodded gently, and in cryptic fashion, "Remember, Oh Iara, that the truest wish that cannot be granted by magic, is love. Not the love that comes from spells or promises, but the love that is free, unconditional, and shared between souls. That is the wish you must make with your heart, and not your mind."

Without another word, Uriel mounted his noble horse. His eyes never left hers, and with a final glance, he urged the beast into motion, the sound of the horses hooves fading into the evening. Iara remained, standing beneath the clouds.

Tomorrow's full moon would quite possibly mark their final moment together.

On the following eve, as the full moon cast its silvery glow upon the land, Iara found herself anxiously tucking her nieces into their beds. However, a strange emptiness was felt inside her heart. Though her body was now filled with life... a child, her soul felt lonely. An unmistakable tension gripped her, for she knew this night bore the truth of her final wish, one that would alter the very course of her destiny.

The hour approached when she would venture forth to manifest her last desire, a decision that both excited, and stirred dread within her. With a candle held firmly in her hand, just as she had done countless times before, she moved past eleven minutes of the eleventh hour and stepped into the darkness of the jungle. Not a glimmer of light broke the dense vegetation, save for the faint glow of her candle. The air was alive with the sounds of the night, and the distant, eerie calls of strange creatures hidden from sight. Each step she took urged her onward into the unknown.

And lo, upon reaching the sacred place that had been her altar several nights past, Iara grew anxious. She sought the form of Uriel amidst the darkness. Yet his calming shadow eluded her. Each silhouette that moved in the background seemed to bear his appearance, but alas, it was but a mere figment of her imagination.

Without the existence of his presence, she knelt on the ground, the coolness pressing against her as she placed the candlestick before her, its warm flame softly illuminating her features. "Uriel, where art thou?" she called thrice.

Only silence answered her. Where could he be? The unease swelled within, a persistent whisper that he might not come at all. "Uriel! Uriel!" she yelled out, her voice now filled with urgency. "Grant me that which I seek! You promised to be here. Where are you? I have come for my final wish!"

Oh Uriel, hear my plea... I wish....

As the truth dawned upon her, Iara began to grasp the weight of Uriel's words from the day before. He had known her all too well, though only a short time had passed since their paths first crossed. In his presence, she had opened her heart, laid bare her vulnerabilities, and he had bestowed upon her all that she desired... now only to vanish into the darkness like a wisp of smoke.

A profound realisation struck her, and with it came crushing despair. Her body crumpled to the earth, fingers gripping the ground with such intensity that the very blades of grass were torn from their roots. Tears cascaded down her cheeks.

"Where art thou?" she cried out into the night. "You have lied to me! I have returned as you did promise. Uriel!" The name burst forth from her lips, longing for the one who had become both her light, and her tormentor. And suddenly, his words seemed to echo across her mind:

Call to me, and I shall heed,

Your every want, your every need,

Your heart's truest wish, I shall grant,

Anything you desire, just take my hand,

Yet there is only one, a wish forbidden,

Not every wish can be fulfilled and written

It was only now that she understood what Uriel had meant, and perhaps that is why, he never appeared.

From a distance, Chimba, the warrior of his people, crouched with his companions, concealed among the thick bushes, their eyes wide with bewilderment at the sight of Iara, alone in the darkness, sobbing before an ancient tree.

"What is she doing?" Chimba's companion whispered. "She has been acting strangely since you had slept with her."

"I know not," Chimba replied, his face riddled with concern. "It cannot be my doing, can it not? She has carried this oddness for weeks. Some say she visits this very tree each night, pleading to it for a final wish. Yet she never utters it, for she fears she may never attain it, what a dilemma."

"Why would that be?" his friend asked, confusion on his face.

"Because" Chimba said slowly, "perhaps it is... a wish forbidden..."

"And what may that wish be?" his friend pressed, yet Chimba fell silent. The group grew quiet, their attention fixated on Iara, who continued to weep in the shadows, while the warriors looked on...

"I hope that you have found the experience truly enjoyable. Kindly reveal the inscription to offer your thoughts."

REVEAL THE INSCRIPTION